"For Rosie, Alfie, Joe, Tom & Will."

Hi5

STEVE

Published by

www.hellygog.co.uk

This is a story, that you love to hear,

It’s all about the Pyjama Farmer my dears.

“YES, YES mum, it’s our favourite PLEASE!”

Well, settle down and listen to me.

The Sandman

You all believe in Santa, Jack Frost blue,

the Sandman, Easter Bunny, Tooth Fairy too.

But there were other creatures, from this time,

and on my hands, I can count at least nine!

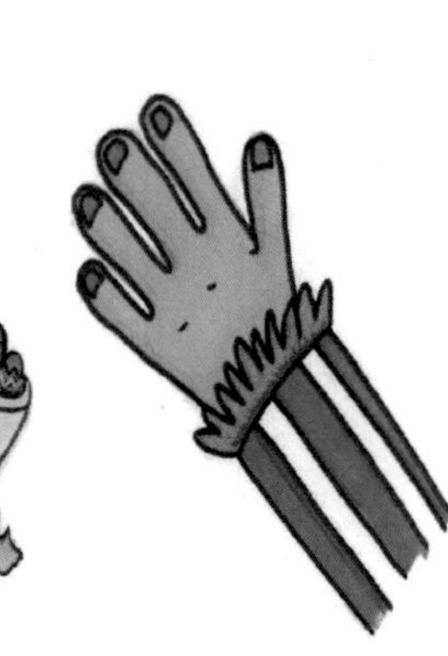

The Easter Bunny

The Tooth Fairy

There were Trolls and Gnomes and Rinky Dink Po,

Dragons and Unicorns, white as snow.

Thrapple Bears and Rankel Sneep,

the Hossle Back Snoot and the Three Legged Meep.

Magical hair,
orange and gold,
skin so blue,
it looks quite cold.
A smile with teeth,
almost fangs,
a long, long nose
and great big hands.

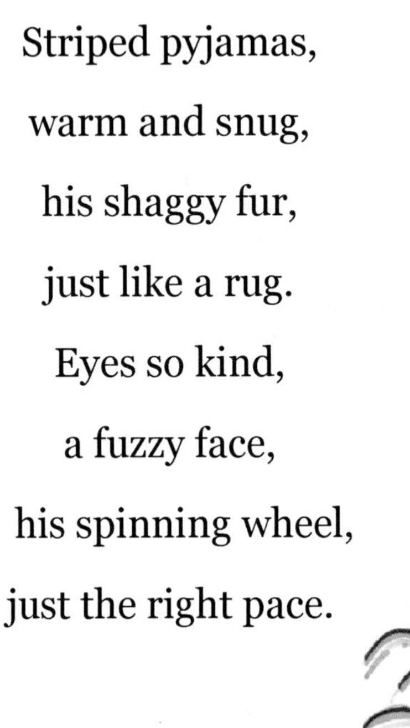

Striped pyjamas,

warm and snug,

his shaggy fur,

just like a rug.

Eyes so kind,

a fuzzy face,

his spinning wheel,

just the right pace.

PF

From cloud to cloud, dropping golden threads,

putting smiles back on weary heads.

He sounds quite cool, I hear you say,

so, why did he have to go away?

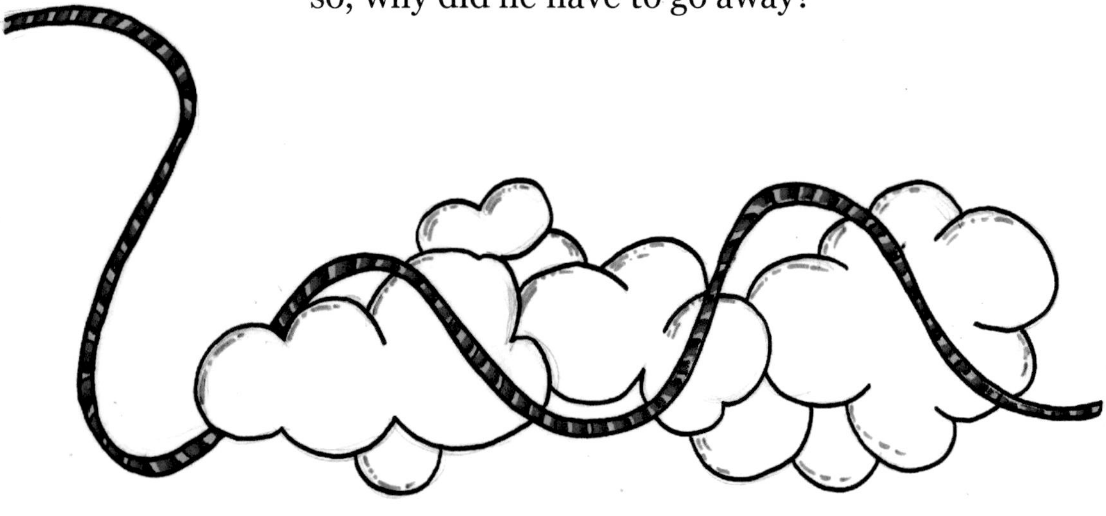

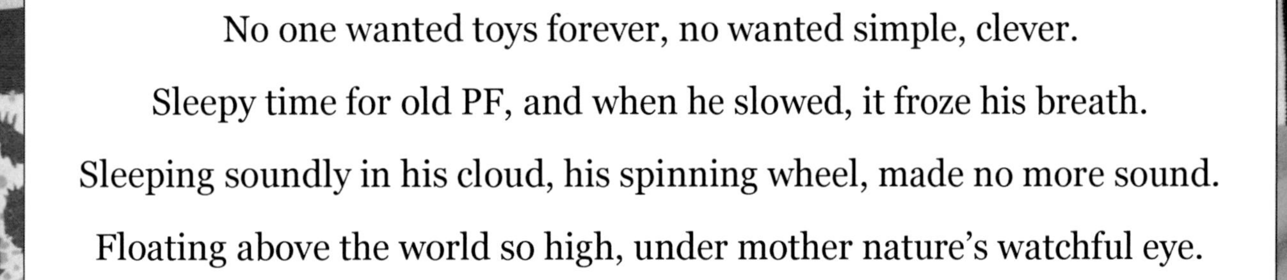

No one wanted toys forever, no wanted simple, clever.

Sleepy time for old PF, and when he slowed, it froze his breath.

Sleeping soundly in his cloud, his spinning wheel, made no more sound.

Floating above the world so high, under mother nature’s watchful eye.

It started to twitch and move about,

and then the Pyjama Pet, gave a shout.

“HELLO JOE, HELLO MUM!

I’M ALIVE! LET’S HAVE SOME FUN!”

With this miracle

something stirred,

a great big sigh,

from ruffled fur.

PF waking up,

looked in the mirror,

his scruffy face,

looking thinner.

His mane, now long, down to the floor,

he cut it off, just like before.

Then gathering up his precious hair,

He began to spin, without a care.

The more she made,

the stronger he grew,

his nose began to glow,

bright blue.

Everyone loved

Pyjama Pets,

and just think, pyjamas,

don't need vets!

From up above, PF looked down,

his spinning wheel, spun around and round.

More thread for mum, from his fine crown,

turning frowns upside down.

As mother sewed and things got better, PF left his cloud forever.

He just appeared, one dull day, the Pyjama Farmer in Darnaway.

Mother smiled, “So the stories true!” “Yes! he said, because of you!”

“You found my thread and used it well,

my story YES! There’s more to tell!”

Mother smiled and let him in,

"Stay with us!"

with that he grinned.

And now he lives at 54,

A great big house,

with three front doors.

54

Rosie, Alfie, Joe and Tom,

Baby Will, still to come.

Mum and Dad, that makes seven,

not everyone's idea of heaven.

And now with PF under the roof,

to throw away, there's no excuse.

So, remember children, wait a bit!

Keep your clothes, when they don't fit.

PJ's, onesies, baby grows,
blankies, sookies, nighties....NO!
Keep them safe, and soon one day,
the Pyjama Farmer,
might come your way!
BABY GIRL
BOY

THE END
or is it ?

DEDICATED TO "HELLYGOG" - HELEN SIMMS. ALWAYS MISSED, NEVER FORGOTTEN.

If you would like more information on how to join the

Pyjama Farmer Team, *or how YOU !can make*

Or get your own Pyjama Pet, then visit us at-

Hellygog.co.uk

Jude & Steve Simms have 5 children, and own & run "Hellygog".

Hellygog is an arts and crafts shop, based at Logie Steading,

in Moray, Scotland, on the banks of the picturesque River Findhorn.

Jude is a physiotherapist, turned textile artist.

Steve is a trained artist, & he is also a staff nurse.

"Thanks for reading this book, we hope you enjoyed it. We look forward to bringing you, more stories in the future."

Jude & Steve

Made in the USA
Columbia, SC
11 April 2017